Chapter One

Hunter Marks was high in the sky. The dino-bot he had made was flying faster and faster. Hunter was sliding down its wing. He was going to fall off.

The wind pushed hard against
Hunter's body. His hands hurt
and his arms shook.

Hunter gripped his d-bot's
handles.

'I won't fall off,' he cried. He
pulled his legs onto the wing.
'I made you and I *will* stay on
you. I have to catch that dino!'

Hunter needed a plan – and
fast.

Hunter saw the d-bot's remote. But it was hanging by a cord under the bot's body. The wind was blowing it around wildly. *I need that remote to control my d-bot*, Hunter thought. *Can I get it without letting go of the bot?*

The d-bot climbed even higher.
It's now or never, Hunter thought,
kneeling on the wing. He let go
of one of the d-bot's handles.
His knees went out from under
him. The wind lifted Hunter up.
He thought he might blow away.

'**Aaargh!**' he cried.

Hunter grabbed the handle again. Then he flattened his body against the bot. *This feels safer,* he thought. *I'll try to creep along the wing a bit. Then I'll be able to reach the cord of the remote.*

When Hunter was ready, he let go of the left handle. He quickly grabbed the cord. 'Got it!' he said, pulling the remote up. Then he pushed the button to slow his d-bot.

As the bot's speed began to drop, the wind dropped too.

But Hunter didn't dare move.
He was still high up in the sky.
He kept his finger on the button
until the bot's wings were barely
flapping.

'Phew,' Hunter cried, sitting back
on the bot. 'Now I need to
learn to fly this d-bot better!'

Hunter clipped the remote to the front of his tool belt. Now it wouldn't fall again.

'Ms Stegg was right,' he said, shaking out his hands. 'It's much harder flying for real. Flying a dino-bot in the game at D-Bot Squad base was easy.'

'Okay, d-bot,' Hunter said.
'I know how fast you can go.
Let's see what else you can do.
I need to ride you like a pro!'

Hunter looked down at the
remote. 'So, not so fast this
time, d-bot,' he said. Then he
gently tapped the speed button.

Hunter and the d-bot began moving faster again. *There's a ptero out there somewhere,* Hunter thought. *I need to catch it safely. I can't let Ms Stegg and Dino Corp down.*

Chapter Two

Hunter flew his d-bot over the city, looking down as he did. Everything looked so small from up there.

He dived down a little lower.

Hunter flew fast and slow. He climbed and dropped. He flew backwards and forwards. He even did a few spins. 'I knew I'd learn to fly you,' he cried to the d-bot.

Now Hunter had control of his d-bot, he began to think about the ptero.

Pteros loved eating fish, he thought. *Perhaps it's hungry! Maybe I should go fishing! I could dive down and use my d-bot's beak to catch some fish. They could come in handy.*

Hunter turned the d-bot towards the sea. He swooped and soared. It was fun.

'I'm flying,' Hunter said. 'I can't believe I'm doing this. Those kids back at school didn't believe I saw a real ptero. They'd never believe this. But who cares! I'm really flying.'

Just then, the sky filled with a terrible noise.

'Squuaark! Wreeeeeekk! Squuaark!'

'What's that?' Hunter said, looking around. 'It's hurting my ears.'

'Squuaark! Wreeeeeekk! Squuaark!'

All at once, a huge flock of
seagulls flew at Hunter.

'Aaargh!' he cried as he tried to
steer the d-bot through them.
'I'm getting covered in bird poo.
This is *so gross*!'

**'Squuaark! Wreeeeeekk!
Squuaark!'**

The gulls were flying very fast. Some flew right at the d-bot. Hunter had to work hard not to hit them.

These birds are scared, he thought. *Really scared.*

'Squuaark! Wreeeeeekk! Squuaark!'

Once the flock passed, Hunter saw where they'd come from.

I need to go to that island! he thought. *But first, some fishing. It'll get rid of this stinky poo, too.*

Hunter opened his d-bot's beak and took a deep breath. Then down they went. **Splash!**

Hunter flew his d-bot back out of the water. 'I'm glad my uniform is quick-dry! Dino Corp has thought of everything.'

Hunter looked at the bot's beak. It was filled with fish. 'Ha! I did it. Food for a hungry dinosaur. Perfect!'

The island loomed up ahead.
It was covered in trees and rocks.
Perched on the highest rock was
Hunter's target, the ptero.

'There it is!' cried Hunter. 'This
will be easy. I might hang on
to my fish for now.'

Hunter's plan was to sneak up on the ptero. Next, he would open his d-bot's hatch. The hood stored inside would fall over the dino's head. Then he'd drop onto its back and wrap the bot's wings around it.

Just like he'd done in the game back at D-Bot Squad's base.

Chapter Three

Hunter flew closer to the island. He could see the ptero clearly now. It stood on its short legs, its wings down. It was resting in the sun.

Hunter dropped his d-bot's speed and floated in the sky. *I'll just look at it for a bit before I catch it,* he thought. *Wow! A real live ptero. It's just like in my books!*

Hunter wished he had his mum's phone. Then he could take a photo.

But Hunter knew he had a job to do for D-Bot Squad. *No photos allowed anyway*, he thought. *This is top-secret work, to help keep the dinosaurs safe.*

He glided his d-bot silently towards the ptero.

But Hunter hadn't thought about the sun.

The sun was behind Hunter and his d-bot. It cast long shadows in front of them. Their shadows. And, as they got closer, their shadows fell over the dinosaur.

Oh no! Hunter thought. *Our shadows have beaten us to the ptero. So much for sneaking up on it.*

The ptero turned and opened its
mouth wide.

'**Screeeeeooooowwkk!**'

And with a flap of its wings, it
was gone.

Hunter stared after the dinosaur, eyes wide. 'I thought it would eat me! Let's go and get it, d-bot!'

Hunter found the ptero on the other side of the island. It was on a tiny beach. Its claws were busy pushing mud and broken shells into a pile.

'Yes – found you!' Hunter cried. He hit the remote button to open his d-bot's jaws.

The fish fell from his d-bot's mouth to the ground. Hunter flew behind a huge pile of rocks and waited.

The dinosaur sniffed and turned. It stomped towards the pile of fish. It bent its head and began to eat.

Hunter acted quickly this time. He landed softly on the ptero's back. It let out a cry.

'Screeeeeoooowwkk!'

'It's okay,' Hunter said, wrapping his d-bot's wings around the ptero. 'I won't hurt you. I'm here to help.' He hadn't needed the hood after all.

Hunter looked at his d-band's teleport button. It was time to send this dinosaur back to its safe, secret home.

He carefully rested a hand on its neck. It felt like soft leather. *I wish I could keep you*, he thought. *You're so awesome!*

Hunter pushed the teleport button. A ray shot out from the d-band and hit the ptero.

The dinosaur began to vanish.
Hunter flew his d-bot off its
back.

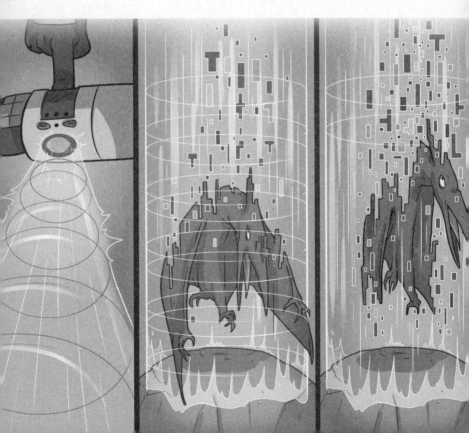

The ptero was gone. 'We did it, d-bot,' he said. 'Too easy! Time to go back to D-Bot Squad base.'

But as Hunter went to press the button, a massive shadow fell over him.

Chapter Four

Hunter looked up as the
shadow passed. 'It's a
quetzalcoatlus,' Hunter gasped.
'I think they're the biggest
flying dinos ever. And I'm
seeing one for real!'

Hunter knew quite a bit about this dino. His mind worked fast.

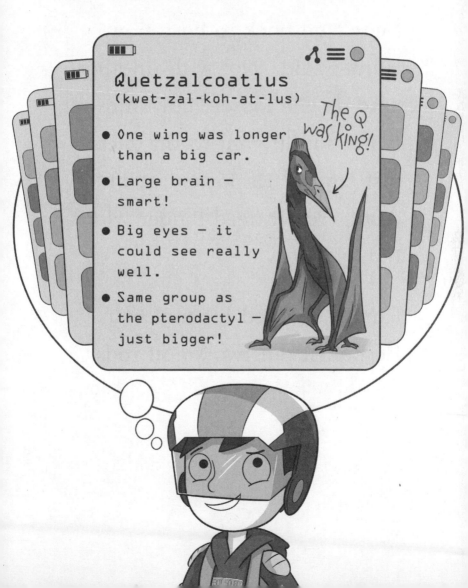

'I can't go back to base now,'
Hunter said. 'Not with another
dino on the loose. That dinosaur
is not so different to the ptero –
just bigger.' He looked at his
d-bot. 'You'll need longer wings,
though.'

Hunter checked his tool belt.
He pulled out two small rods.

'Expando-rods! These will work!' he said.

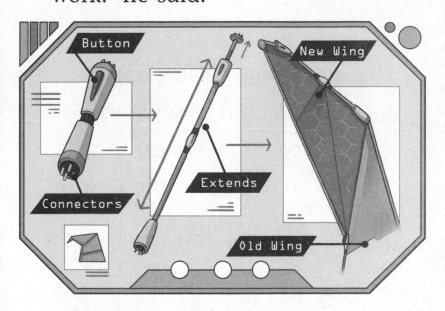

Hunter used the screwdriver to open his d-bot's wings. He fitted the rods between the panels. Then he pressed the 'expand-o-go' button on the rods.

The new wing panels popped open and locked into place. 'That's ace!' Hunter said. 'It will be easy rounding up the Q with these massive wings.'

Hunter stood back and checked out his d-bot. *Is there anything else I could add?* he wondered.

A loud noise broke through Hunter's thoughts.

Clap! Wooooshh! Clap! Wooooshh!

He watched as the dinosaur flew over the island and out to sea. 'It sure is huge,' Hunter said, climbing onto his d-bot.

The dinosaur made a turn. It was heading back towards the island. 'It's got such a long neck,' Hunter said. 'It might be taller than a giraffe when it stands!'

Hunter needed to catch it quickly.

As Hunter grabbed his d-bot's remote, his d-band lit up. It was Ms Stegg. 'Well done, Hunter,' her voice boomed through the d-band's speaker.

'The pterodactyl is safe in the park – but where are you? You should be back here at D-Bot Squad base.'

Hunter pushed the button to speak on his d-band. 'There's a quetzalcoatlus out here,' he said. 'It's sort of the same as the ptero, only bigger. I can catch it easily.

'I still have the hood in my
d-bot's hatch,' Hunter added.
'I'll catch it just like I caught
the ptero in the game.'

But Ms Stegg wasn't so sure.
'You'll need help. A quetzalcoatlus
is too strong for one D-Bot
Squad member to handle.'

But I'm the only D-Bot Squad member, Hunter thought. *Aren't I...?*

'Wait in a safe place. I will send someone else to you,' Ms Stegg added.

Hunter drew a sharp breath. *So there is someone else,* he thought. He kicked the rocks at his feet.

I thought I was the only D-Bot Squad member. I thought I was the only one who could do this job. I don't want anyone else messing things up!

I don't need help!

'Hunter, are you still there?'

Ms Stegg's voice snapped Hunter out of his thoughts. He took a few deep breaths and said, 'I'm here and I've got this. I don't need help.'

Just then the big dinosaur swooped to the ground.

It landed next to the mound of mud and shells the ptero had built.

Hunter spoke softly into his d-band's speaker. 'It's just landed, not too far away from me. I'll teleport it soon. Over and out.'

Chapter Five

Hunter silently watched the dinosaur. It was digging in the mound of mud and shells with its long beak. *Okay, I'll take off super quietly*, he thought. *Then I'll fly over it and drop the hood.*

But before Hunter could take off, the dinosaur turned. It stared at Hunter with its big, hungry eyes.

'Uh-oh!' Hunter said, hitting the start button on his d-bot's remote. 'Let's go!'

The dinosaur charged at Hunter just as his d-bot left the ground.

Up in the sky, Hunter heard massive claps right behind him.

Flap! Flap! Flap! Flap!

'It's chasing me!' Hunter cried. 'This is all wrong. I'm meant to be the chaser.'

Hunter pressed down hard on the speed button.

His d-bot's wings worked harder and faster. But not fast enough. 'It's gaining on me,' Hunter cried.

As the dinosaur closed in, he hit the button to drop speed. His d-bot suddenly dropped from the sky. Hunter felt like he was falling.

As they dropped, the dinosaur flew over them.

'Qs are too big to turn fast,' Hunter said. 'I don't think they can turn their neck and head, either.'

Hunter pulled his d-bot up higher again. *I did it! Now we're behind it*, he thought.

Hunter was gaining on the dinosaur.
Just a little bit closer! Then I'll drop the hood on it.

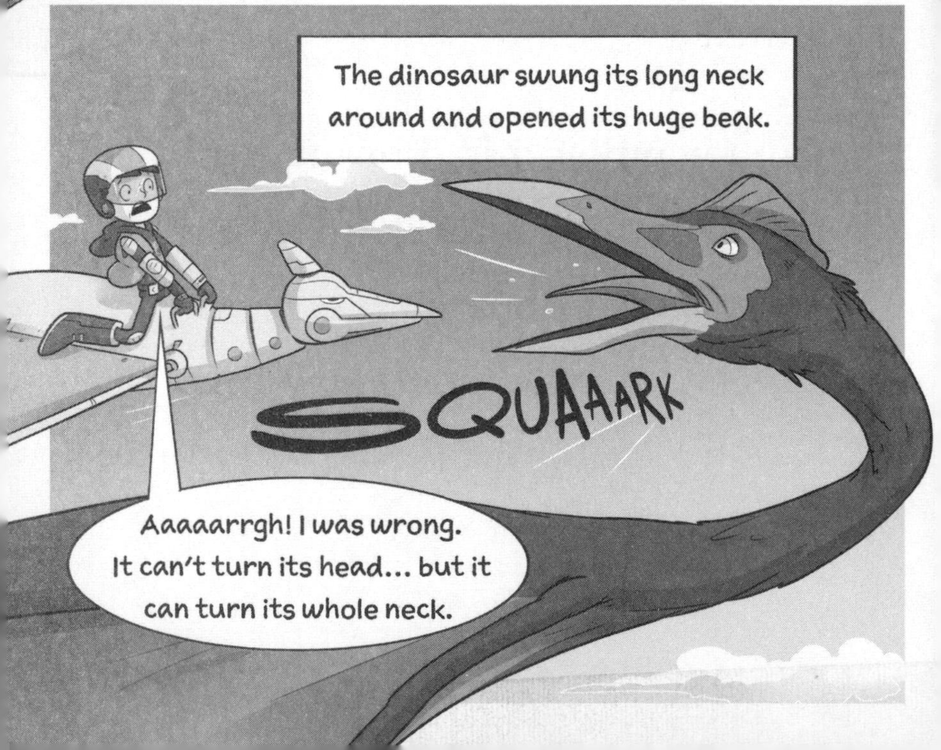
The dinosaur swung its long neck around and opened its huge beak.
SQUAAARK
Aaaaarrgh! I was wrong. It can't turn its head... but it can turn its whole neck.

Hunter landed his d-bot on the island's tiny beach and looked up. The dinosaur was coming after him again. 'It's okay,' he said to himself. 'I want it to land. My d-bot can take off faster than it can.'

Hunter had a plan. He would wait until the dinosaur was close enough. Then he would quickly fly up onto its back and catch it.

The dinosaur hit the ground running. It charged at Hunter. Hunter stayed still.

Come a little bit closer, Hunter thought. *That's it...*

Hunter's finger twitched on the take-off button, but he didn't press it down.

The dinosaur slowed as it closed in on him.

'Now!' Hunter cried. He pressed down hard on the take-off button.

Hunter was in the air in no time. He flew up over the head of the dinosaur. Then he dropped the hood.

'Got you!' called Hunter as the hood covered the dinosaur's head. 'I can't wait to tell Ms Stegg that I've caught you!

But just as Hunter went to land on the dinosaur's back, it lifted its wings. Then it threw its head back. The hood fell to the ground. The dinosaur's head smashed into Hunter's d-bot.

Hunter's d-bot crashed to the ground. Hunter went flying over its head. He landed on his back in the sand.

The dinosaur opened its massive beak and let out a cry.

'Sqquuaaaarrrk!'

Chapter Six

The dinosaur stomped its feet.
Hunter felt the ground shake.
I need to hide, he thought,
crawling quickly behind his
d-bot.

Hunter peered through the gap between his d-bot's neck and the ground. All he could see was the dino's big feet. It hadn't turned around.

Maybe it's forgotten about me, Hunter thought. *I hope you still work, d-bot. We need to get out of here, fast.*

Hunter ran his hand along his d-bot's neck, looking for the remote. *It was pulled from my tool belt when I fell*, he thought. *It must be under the d-bot's head.*

Hunter lifted the bot's head as quietly as he could.

As Hunter pulled the remote free, he tapped the start button. Nothing happened.

Great, now what? Maybe I could have used a bit of help, after all, he thought.

Just then, the dinosaur turned its long neck towards his d-bot.

Hunter peeked out from behind the d-bot. *Don't see me,* he thought. *Don't smell me. Don't even think about coming this way.*

Hunter held his breath and kept as still as possible. And then he sneezed.

The dinosaur opened its long beak and let out another cry.

'Sqquuuaaaaarrrrrk!'

It lifted off from the ground
and flew at Hunter.

Hunter got to his feet and ran,
but the dinosaur was too quick.

The dinosaur snatched Hunter
up with one of its claws. The
other claw grabbed his d-bot.
Then it flew off into the sky.

Will Hunter and
his d-bot get away?
Read Book 3,
Double Trouble, to find out!